First published 2018 by Mabecron Books Ltd,
Bristol Orchard, St Mellion, Saltash, Cornwall, PL12 6RQ.

Illustrated by Fiona Rose. Designed by Keryn Bibby.
Typeset in Minion Pro. Printed in Malaysia.
ISBN 978 0 9955028 5 7

The Garden Giant

Fiona Rose

The Giant first appeared as a shape in the storm clouds.
The townspeople didn't see her; they were too busy trying to save
their tiny town from being swept away by the terrible storm.
They were desperate for help.

Without words she summoned her silent strength.
Her feet dropped like anchors as her arms made
a giant ark around the town, shielding them from
the pounding waves and howling wind.

She filled her lungs with enough air to launch a thousand ships and blew into the angry sky.
The clouds parted and the storm hushed.
In the growing silence a new sound could be heard...

It was the townspeople, joyfully cheering her.

Children danced
Fishermen threw their nets high in the air
And a rainbow painted itself across the sky like a party banner.

The small town gave the Giant its biggest welcome!

With their experienced hands, the men and women carefully untangled the Giant's knotty, net-filled hair.

They unwove the seaweed from her fingers
Plucked the barnacles from her knees
And cleaned between her jumbo toes.

They gathered the torn sail cloth left over from
the storm and neatly sewed the seams together.
When the Giant was dry, they dressed her.

She felt beautiful.
She was….

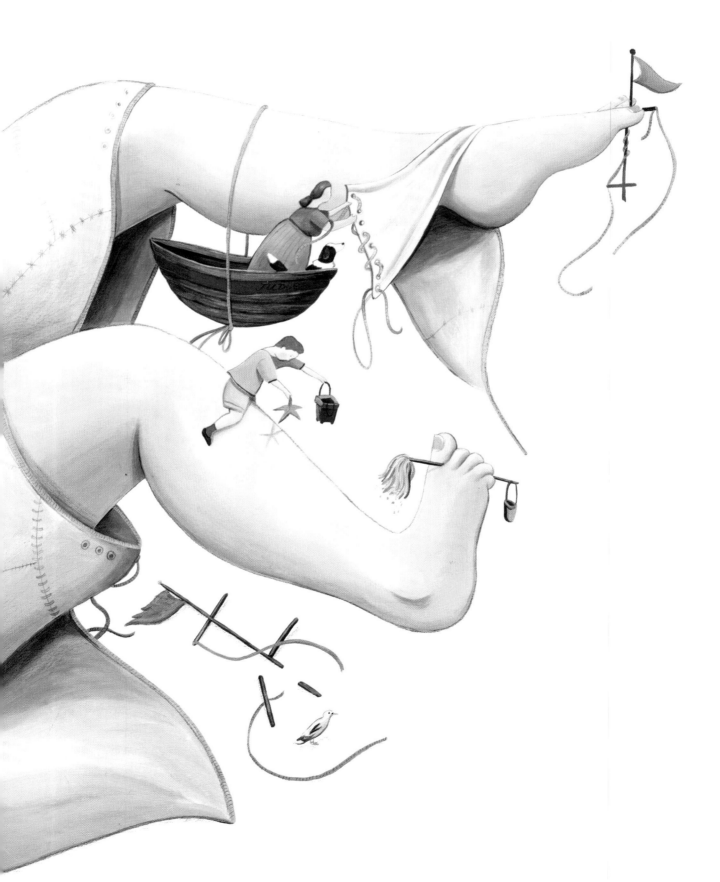

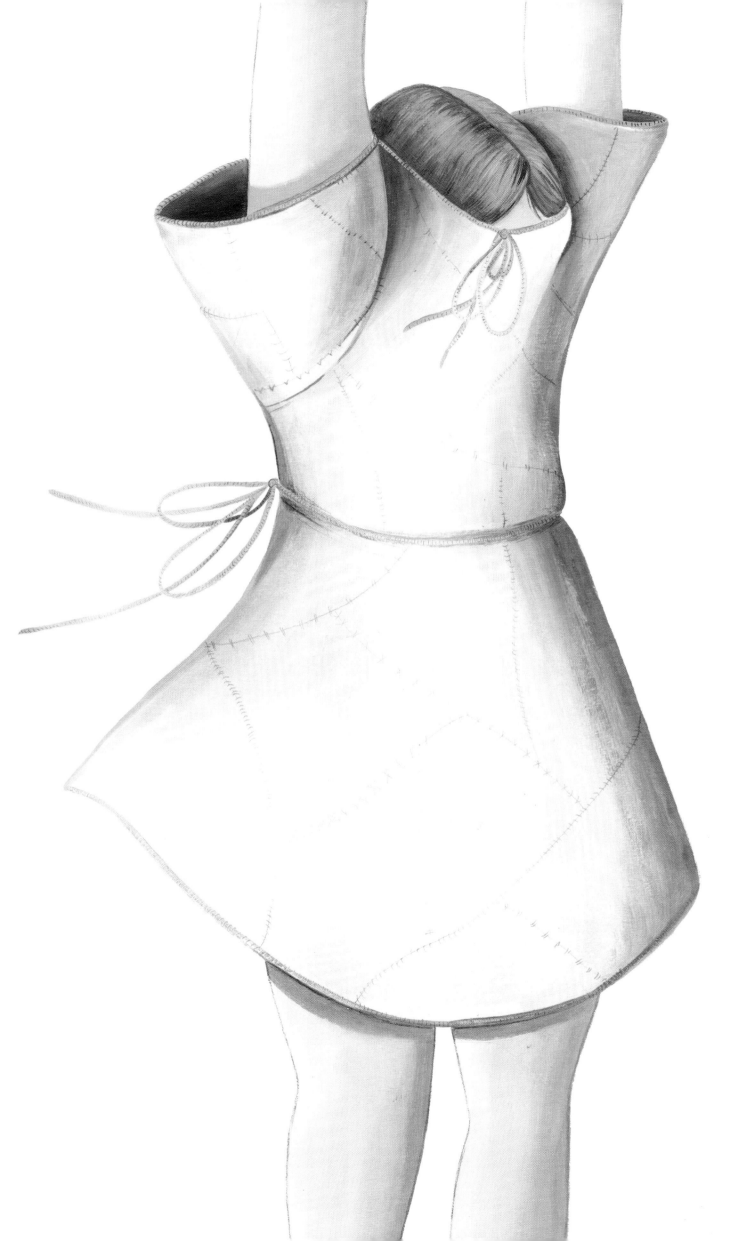

Out of nowhere a deep rumbling sound shook the street.
The thunder seemed to be coming from the Giant's tummy.

'You must be hungry?' asked the townsfolk,
who were already hurrying to their kitchens.
'Yes, a little,' she replied.

Every cupboard was emptied
Every vegetable peeled
And every oven roared.

A wondrous smell soon filled the air as a fine feast
was prepared.

When all the food was eaten,
and every crumb was gone,
slumber crept across the harbour.

The people began to wonder
where the Giant might sleep.

'YAAAWWWWWWN'

Her gaping mouth gave them an idea.
'We know a perfect place for you to rest'
they chimed.

They led her carefully down a rocky path 'til they reached
a secret cavern. It was dark and cold and as much as
she tried, the Giant could not get comfortable there.
'Hmmm,' the townspeople wondered long and hard.

They travelled to the very edge of the
pier, where a lonely light beckoned them.
'Our lighthouse has been looking for a keeper
for a long time,' they said, smiling up at her.
'It looks cosy,' said the Giant.

And it was.

But as much as she tried to make
herself at home, she was just too big.

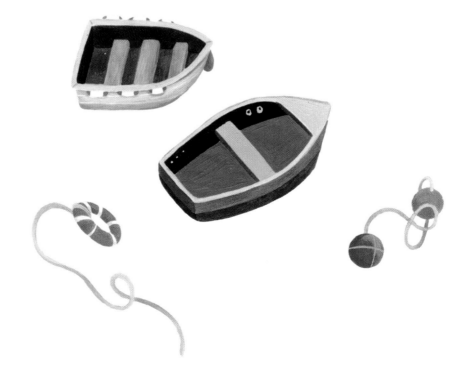

With a heavy sigh, she began to wonder whether
she belonged here at all. 'Seaside towns are no place
for giants,' she whispered to herself, as her gaze was
drawn to the beam from the lighthouse.

It swept across the horizon towards the land.
She blinked, then blinked again. A mighty tree
became visible in the far distance, 'Perhaps I'm
not the only giant here after all?'

Through the darkness, the Giant made
her way to the top of the hill. She stepped over a large
wall and entered into a land of giant trees and plants.

She listened to the sounds around her:
Scratching insects too small to see
Night-time whispers from weeds and flowers
Trees breathing soundlessly.

Amongst the
sounds she could also hear
the crinkle of dry dead leaves and
the creaking sigh of long fallen oaks.
It seemed as if the garden had been
left alone for a very long time. It had
become overgrown, forgotten and
neglected. The garden spoke to her
without words. She knew it was
asking for her help.

With hands as strong as ploughs,
the Giant tended the garden.

She scooped up the debris,
peeled back the brambles
and made room for new seeds to grow.
She uprooted the old,
straightened the weary
and nurtured the new.

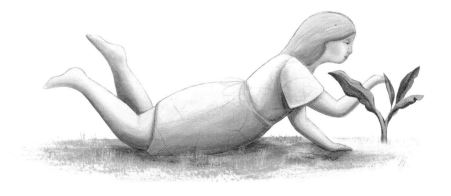

She worked tirelessly throughout the long night.

Leaf by leaf, the garden began to heal.
And so, in the morning sun, it sang.

The Giant couldn't believe that she was
surrounded by so much magnificence.

She weeded and watered her garden
She breathed the scents and the colours
And listened to the birds and the insects.

But even amongst all the beauty of the garden,
still she felt that something was missing.

She looked down towards the little town, remembering
her friends and the night of the terrible storm.
She closed her eyes for a moment and when
she opened them she saw the townspeople
climbing the hill towards the garden.

They were happy that the Giant had found a place
she liked. But they had not forgotten her, the way they
had forgotten their garden.

And neither had they forgotten their promise
to find her a comfortable place to sleep.